CONTENTS

Published 2008
Published by Pedigree Books LTD,
Beech Hill House • Walnut Gardens • Exeter, Devon EX4 4DH • books@pedigreegroup.co.uk
Kung Fu Panda ™ & © 2008 DreamWorks Animation L.L.C.

MEET THE

MASTER OOGWAY

Around 1000 years ago, Master Oogway is too old to fight and so he now acts as the valley's spiritual leader. He can often be found under the Peach Tree of Heavenly Wisdom and sprinkles its blossom petals in the Jade Palace's pool each morning.

PO

Po spends his days working in his father's restaurant, but is sure that there is more to life than making noodles. His dream is to meet kung fu stars the Furious Five and when he is unexpectedly chosen to defend his valley from its biggest threat in twenty years, he will finally get a chance to fight alongside his heroes.

MR PING

Mr Ping lives, eats and sleeps noodles in the restaurant that has been in his family for generations. The only problem is that he expects his son Po to do the same! His signature dish is a Secret Ingredient Soup, but he can only reveal what that secret ingredient is when his son is ready to take over.

CHARACTERS

MASTER TIGRESS

The strongest and boldest of the Furious Five, Tigress is a true kung fu hero: high-achieving and fearless. She'll do anything to save the day, except believe in Po – she thinks he's a joke (and not a very funny one at that). No opponent scares her, not even the notorious Tai Lung.

MASTER CRANE

Crane is the peacekeeper of the group, always keeping a cool head to manage the clashing personalities of the other masters. Although he will do all he can to avoid a conflict, he has the skill to win a fight if necessary. He is the first master to warm to Po... once he has tasted his home cooking!

MASTER SHIFU

Although this stern kung fu master has trained the best warriors in China, he thinks that transforming a flabby, noodle-making panda into a skilful fighter is beyond even him! When the valley comes under threat, however, he discovers that Po is not the only one who needs to learn a thing or two about life.

MASTER MANTIS

He may be the smallest of the Five by far, but what Mantis lacks in size, he makes up for in strength and speed. He has a mean temper, too, and will literally kick off at the slightest insult. Nothing can strike fear into his tiny heart!

MASTER MONKEY

Whilst he is friendly, playful and enthusiastic, Monkey possesses stunning martial arts skills and agility. He laughs easily and enjoys the unique spectacle of a giant panda trying to do kung fu. The staff is his weapon of choice and he finds a bout with Po especially entertaining!

MASTER VIPER

This vain and stunning warrior can be a charming flirt one minute and then a deadly opponent the next. Her astonishing flexibility allows her to avoid blows before moving in with her own deadly strike. She does have a soft centre, though, and worries that Po will get hurt during training.

CHARACTERS

TAI LUNG

Once upon a time, everyone believed that this huge snow leopard was the greatest fighter ever. Only Oogway saw the darkness that was in his heart and refused him the top honour of becoming the Dragon Warrior. The rampage that followed ended with Tai Lung being locked in Chorh-Gom prison.

ZENG

This jumpy goose is the palace envoy entrusted with taking a warning message from Shifu to the prison after Oogway's vision that Tai Lung will escape. Often a messenger with bad news, Zeng is a hard-pressed servant who still tries to do his best at all times.

COMMANDER VACHIR

As Commander at Chorh-Gom, Vachir is the mastermind behind the seemingly inescapable prison that was built to house a single inmate. He is confident that his unit is secure and is offended by the suggestion that it may not be. But all it takes is one slip-up in the shape of a feather…

DRAGON WARRIOR

There once lived a legendary kung fu warrior who travelled the land in search of worthy foes... and perhaps a bit of lunch. As he took bamboo and tea in a bar one afternoon, a gang burst in and surrounded him. "I see you like to chew," sneered the gang leader. "Maybe you should chew on my fist!" He slammed his fist down on the table to make his point.

The warrior said nothing. This was because his mouth was full... so he swallowed. "Enough talk," he said at last, like a true hero. "Let's fight. SHASHABOOEY!" WHAM! The courageous warrior delivered a punch that sent the whole gang flying. They flailed around, blinded by this kung fu master's pure awesomeness. "My eyes!" cried one. "He's too awesome!" exclaimed another.

"And attractive!" added an onlooker, as others swooned around her. "How can we repay you?" asked another in wonder. "There is no charge," the warrior solemnly replied, "for awesomeness, or attractiveness." But at that moment, one hundred assassins appeared and crowded round him menacingly. Then a thousand ninjas. "KABLOOEY!" The bar roof exploded and a cloud of ninjas erupted into the sky as the warrior spun like a tornado, knocking them all down. No matter how many foes he faced, they were no match for his bodacity. The biggest heroes in China, the Furious Five, bowed in respect to this great master. Monkey even said they should hang out together. But hanging out would have to wait, for the ten thousand demons of Demon Mountain were moving in for an attack.

Bravely facing the sea of bandits, the Five prepared for attack. The warrior pulled out a shiny green sword, his trusty Jade Avenger, and brandished it as he leaped off the mountain... onto his bedroom floor. The big, round panda gazed at the blanket tangled around his stout body and at his stubby leg, still stuck in the

"Monkey! Mantis! Crane! Viper! Tigress! Rowrrrr...!" he growled, as he played with the action figures of his heroes.

"Po! Let's go!" Mr Ping was getting impatient now. "You're late!"

"Coming!" In a final gesture, Po picked up his ninja star and threw it at the wall, only for it to bounce off. He picked it up and tried a second time, but still couldn't quite manage to embed it in the wall. Giving up, he took the star and headed downstairs, tripping over his feet and tumbling down to land flat on his face in the kitchen.

"Sorry, Dad," he groaned to a stern goose.

"Sorry doesn't make the noodles," came the rebuke. As Po hauled himself up and set to work, his dad asked what all the noise had been.

"Oh, nothing," said Po. "Just had a crazy dream."

bed. As his head cleared and his kung fu posters came into focus, he let out a big sigh. It had all been a dream. He tried to kick himself to his feet, but his belly was too worthy a foe.

"Po! Get up!" his father called. "What are you doing up there?"

"Uh, nothing!" Po replied, finally getting to his feet with a kung fu stance.

"What were you dreaming about?" asked Mr Ping, chopping vegetables.

"What was I... eh, I was dreaming about, uh…" Po stammered, trying to think of something acceptable, "…noodles."

"Noodles?" Mr Ping was delighted. "You were really dreaming about noodles?"

"Uh, yeah," Po nodded. "What else would I be dreaming about?"

Po handed a bowl to a customer a moment before noticing that his star had fallen in it.

"Careful," he warned. "That soup is... sharp!" The next thing he knew, his dad was giving him a big hug.

"Oh, happy day!" smiled Mr Ping. "My son, finally having the noodle dream! You don't know how long I've been waiting for this moment." He pulled back, having deftly put a noodle apron on his son. "This is a sign, Po!"

Po looked down at the apron.

"A sign of what?" he asked nervously.

"You are almost ready to be entrusted with the secret ingredient of my Secret Ingredient Soup," Mr Ping explained. "Then you will fulfil your destiny and take over the restaurant, just as I took it over from my father, who took it over from his father, who won it in a game of mahjong…"

"Dad, Dad," Po interrupted. "It was just a dream."

"No, it was THE dream," insisted his dad. "We are noodle folk. Broth runs through our veins."

"But didn't you ever, I dunno, want to do something else besides noodles?" To Po's surprise, his dad said he did once think about running away to make tofu, but that was when he was young and crazy.

"We all have our place in this world," Mr Ping added. "Mine is here and yours is out there. Table three is waiting for their soup."

From the restaurant Po would often look into the distance at the Jade Palace, where his idols the Furious Five trained with their master, Shifu. That morning, Shifu had been playing his flute when the Five sprang upon him in an attempt to take him by surprise. He moved at lightning speed, using the flute as a staff to block and deflect their blows until they were all defeated.
"Well done, students... if you were trying to disappoint me," he said sternly. Using the flute as a pointer, he corrected each of the Five's technique.
"Tigress, you need more ferocity; Monkey, greater speed. Crane, height; Viper, subtlety."
Before the master could get to Mantis, a palace goose came running up to him.
"It's Master Oogway," said Zeng. "He wants to see you."

Shifu entered Oogway's candlelit, incense-filled room and bowed before the ancient tortoise, waiting to hear what was wrong. "I have had a vision," Oogway explained. "Tai Lung will return."

"That's impossible," said Shifu, his heartbeat quickening. "He is in prison!"

"Nothing is impossible," Oogway said wisely. As a precaution, Shifu summoned Zeng and ordered him to go at once to the prison.

"Tell them to double the guards, double their weapons... double everything! Tai Lung does not leave that prison."

"Yes, Master Shifu," the goose agreed. Oogway remained calm and turned to the Moon Pool.

"One often meets his destiny on the road he takes to avoid it," he said.

"We have to do something," Shifu began, panic rising within him. "We can't let him take his revenge on the valley! He'll, he'll…"

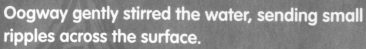

Oogway gently stirred the water, sending small ripples across the surface.

"Your mind is like this water, my friend," he noted, staring into the pool. "When it is agitated, it is difficult to see. But if you allow it to settle, the answer becomes clear."

Shifu watched as the water became still, revealing the reflection of the carved dragon above, a scroll in its mouth.

"The Dragon Scroll..." said Shifu, puzzled.

"It is time," Oogway told him.

"But who is worthy to be trusted with the secret to limitless power?" Shifu asked in astonishment. "To become... the Dragon Warrior?"

Oogway fixed him with a steady gaze.

"I don't know," he confessed.

Po's day was interrupted by the arrival of palace geese with a poster for the restaurant. He peered at it and his eyes widened. "Master Oogway is choosing the Dragon Warrior! Today!" he exclaimed. "Everyone to the Jade Palace – one of the Five is gonna get the Dragon Scroll. We've been waiting a thousand years for this!" Po didn't even care about the bills. He went to catch

up with the crowds, but his father stopped him. "Po! Where are you going?" he asked. "To the... Jade Palace?" Po replied hopefully. "But you're forgetting your noodle cart," Mr Ping pointed out. "The whole valley will be there!" Po wasn't going so that he could sell noodles, but he agreed just to keep the old goose happy.

Po stood with his noodle cart at the bottom of the Palace steps; they seemed to go on forever! He took a deep breath and started to climb. He felt liked he must be almost there, but when he looked up he had barely moved. "We'll bring you back a souvenir," teased a passer-by, overtaking him.

"No," Po said, narrowing his eyes in determination. "I'll bring me back a souvenir."

As he struggled on upwards, he heard a gong sound from the arena. At the very moment he hoisted his body over the last step, laughing jubilantly to himself, the doors to the palace arena were closing.

"Oh, no! No, no, no!" he yelled, jumping up. "Wait! I'm coming!"

平靜

Po banged on the closed doors, but the ceremonial drums inside drowned him out. "Let me in!" he shouted at the top of his voice, trying in vain to be heard above the cheers. He scrabbled up to an open window as Shifu addressed the crowd. "Citizens of the Valley of Peace," the master began. "It is my great honour to present to you... Tigress! Viper! Crane! Monkey! Mantis! The Furious Five!" Po gasped as he got a glimpse of the Five jumping into the middle of the ring before a gust of wind made him wobble and fall to the ground, the window slamming shut. "Warriors, prepare!" ordered Shifu. Po scuttled to a crack in the wall and looked through it. "Peeky-hole!" he said to himself, as Shifu told the Five to be ready for battle.

"Yeah! Woo!" Po said excitedly, seeing Crane spread his wings. "The Thousand Tongues of Fire!" He waited eagerly to see what would happen next, but a spectator inside moved and blocked his view. Was Crane flying? He hurried backwards to peer up into the sky... and fell down the steps.

Po was getting desperate. He karate chopped the door, but only hurt his paw and slumped to the ground. Maybe a pole vault would work? It began well, but Po fell on his back and the pole whipped around to knock him into the arena wall. Even a catapult backfired! The disappointed panda felt like giving up, but then he heard another name: Tigress! He had to see her. "Master Tigress," said Shifu. "Face Iron Ox and his Blades of Death!"

Po grabbed a rope attached to a tree and managed to swing himself up high enough to spot Tigress, but came down again just as she did her move. The spectators fell silent as Oogway spoke: "I sense that the Dragon Warrior is among us." "Citizens of the Valley of Peace," Shifu addressed the crowd. "Master Oogway will now choose... the Dragon Warrior!" "Oh, no!" gasped Po. There was no way he was going to miss this. As the ceremonial drums rolled for the build-up to the most important announcement of all time, he looked around frantically and realised that he had landed in the fireworks tent.

"Yeah!" he grinned. He had a great idea...

WILL PO BE IN TIME TO SEE WHO BECOMES THE DRAGON WARRIOR? FIND OUT ON PAGE 30!

DESIGN A DRAGON SCROLL

THE JADE PALACE'S DRAGON SCROLL HOLDS THE SECRET TO LIMITLESS POWER AND HAS A TRADITIONAL CHINESE DECORATION ON THE BACK. USE YOUR PENS OR PENCILS TO DESIGN YOUR OWN DRAGON SCROLL – YOU CAN MAKE IT RED AND GOLD LIKE THE ORIGINAL OR CREATE A UNIQUE COLOUR COMBINATION OF YOUR OWN!

SEEING STARS

PO IS OFTEN A LITTLE CARELESS WITH HIS NINJA STARS – HE LEAVES THEM ALL OVER THE PLACE! CAN YOU SPOT TEN OF HIS LOST STARS IN THIS PICTURE?

CHECK BOX EACH TIME YOU FIND A NINJA STAR

WHO AM I?

WHICH KUNG FU MASTER IS BEING DESCRIBED HERE? YOU'LL FIND THE ANSWER AT THE BACK OF YOUR ANNUAL.

His home is a palace, served by loyal geese,

That stands overlooking the Valley of Peace.

He once was a warrior but now likes to teach,

His favourite tree is the magical peach

That he planted from seed many centuries ago.

(This master is ancient and much does he know.)

The staff that he carries is made of peach wood,

He created kung fu as a new force for good.

CHOW TIME!

PO MAY NOT WANT TO SPEND THE REST OF HIS LIFE MAKING NOODLES, BUT HE LOVES EATING THEM! HE CAN THROW TOGETHER A NOODLE SALAD FASTER THAN YOU CAN SAY MR PING - WHY DON'T YOU TRY IT, TOO?

YOU'LL NEED:

- 250g COOKED NOODLES
- 2 SPRING ONIONS
- A RED PEPPER
- A HANDFUL OF WASHED BEAN SPROUTS
- 2 TABLESPOONS SOY SAUCE
- 1 TABLESPOON SESAME OIL
- A SPLASH OF LIME JUICE
- A HANDFUL OF SESAME SEEDS

ALL YOU HAVE TO DO IS:

1. Ask a grown-up to finely slice the spring onions and red pepper for you.

2. Mix together the soy sauce, sesame oil and lime juice in a small dish or shake them up in a screw-top jam jar.

3. Put your noodles in a salad bowl and add your bean sprouts, spring onions and red pepper.

4. Pour over the soy dressing and mix together well.

5. Sprinkle over the sesame seeds and enjoy!

 Make eating your noodles even more fun by using chopsticks!

PANDA POWER

EVERYONE KNOWS PO SPENDS MOST OF HIS DAY EATING. IN FACT, PANDAS SPEND ABOUT 12 HOURS A DAY SCOFFING BAMBOO, AS THEY CAN'T DIGEST MUCH OF IT! WANT TO KNOW MORE ABOUT PANDAS? READ ON!

Pandas in the wild have up to 30 different types of bamboo to chomp on. It's still a choice of only bamboo or bamboo, though!

A panda was a prized pet for Chinese emperors long ago. It was believed that the bears warded off evil spirits and natural disasters.

Bamboo makes up 99% of a panda's diet – it eats around 30 kg (62 lb) of the stuff a day!

Newborn pandas are pink and blind, with no fur.

Like all bears, pandas like honey – if they can get their paws on it!

Shifu is a red panda. He eats bamboo, too!

Pandas have an enlarged bone that acts as a thumb for gripping bamboo stems.

Unlike other bears, pandas do not hibernate.

Wild pandas can live to be 25 years old.

Wild pandas are pretty rare. There are around 1600 in total and they are found only in mountainous areas of southwest China.

FU JUICE

PRACTISING KUNG FU MOVES IS THIRSTY WORK! PO LOVES A BAMBOO SHAKE TO KEEP HIM GOING UNTIL HE CAN GET HIS PAWS ON SOME FOOD. TRY OUT SOME OF HIS OTHER THIRST QUENCHERS!

RED DRAGON FIZZ

- 1 litre cranberry and raspberry juice
- 500 ml red grape juice
- 450 ml lemonade or sparkling mineral water
- Orange sherbet for frosting (optional)

1. Put some ice cubes into a 2-litre jug and pour in all the cranberry and raspberry juice.

2. Add the grape juice and top up with fizz.

3. Put a little juice in one saucer and some sherbet in another.

4. Before filling each glass or cup, dip the rim in the juice and then in the sherbet for some fiery frosting!

PANDA POWER SMOOTHIE

- 1 banana
- 200g raspberries
- 1 strawberry yoghurt
- 4 ice cubes

1. Peel the banana and ask a grown-up to help you chop it.

2. Wash the raspberries.

3. Put the banana, raspberries, yoghurt and ice in a blender and ask a grown up to whizz them all up for you until you have a super smoothie!

LEVEL ZERO

Mr Ping came to see how the noodle sales were going. "Po?" he gasped, seeing his son light the fuse on a chair laden with fireworks. "What are you doing?" He tried to blow out the flame. "What does it look like I'm doing?" Po replied. "I'm going to see the Dragon Warrior." Mr Ping didn't understand. Hadn't his son had the noodle dream?

"I lied," Po admitted uneasily. "I don't dream about noodles, Dad!" He clung to the chair and shut his eyes, bracing himself for take-off. "I love kung fuuuuuuuuuu!" When he opened his eyes... he had only toppled to the ground. "Come on, son," said his dad, holding out an apron. "Let's get back to work." "Okay," sighed Po. As he reached out for the apron, BOOM! The rockets ignited and he was blasted into the sky.

Po's chair sped upwards amidst a shower of sparks until the rockets fizzled out and it started to lose power.

"Uh oh..." he groaned, heading down towards the middle of the arena. SMASH! Po landed, sending up a huge cloud of dust. As it cleared, he saw the Five looking down at him, appalled. Strangely, Oogway was smiling and pointing. "What's going on?" mumbled Po. "Oh. Okay. Sorry. I just wanted to see who the Dragon Warrior was."

As he shuffled around in an attempt to get up, Tigress asked Oogway if he was pointing at her. "No, him," he said. Po tried to move out of the way of the tortoise's claw, but it followed him.

Oogway used his staff to hold
up Po's paw for all to see.
"The universe has brought us the
Dragon Warrior!" he declared.
"What?" gasped Po.
"WHAT?" gasped the Five.
And Shifu. And Mr Ping.
The Dragon Warrior had been
announced and the gong was
struck. The crowd went wild,
cheering, screaming and showering
confetti. A palanquin arrived to
take the new hero into the Palace.
"Stop!" cried Shifu. "Wait! Who
told you to..." But Po was swept
up and held aloft by the Palace
Geese, who struggled off with him.
Shifu elbowed his way through the
thronging crowd to Oogway's side.
"Master Oogway, that flabby panda
can't be the answer to... our problem,"
he complained. "You were about to
point at Tigress. That thing fell in front
of her. It was just an accident!"

"There are no accidents," smiled
Oogway. Even the crash of Po falling
through the palanquin didn't change
his thrilled expression. A group of burly
pigs rushed over and hoisted Po, the
palanquin and the geese on to their
shoulders and carried them off.
"Forgive us, Master," Tigress said
to Shifu. "We have failed you."
"No," Shifu shook his head. "If the
panda has not quit by morning,
then I will have failed you."

Po's Dad, the Five and their master stood in the arena, stunned, as the celebration continued around them.

When Zeng reached the frozen mountain into which was carved the fifteen-storey Chorh-Gom prison, he landed clumsily on the ice and slid into the gate. The rhino sentries pointed their spears at the hapless goose. "Wait!" he spluttered. "I bring a message from Master Shifu!" The doors creaked open and he entered nervously to deliver the scroll.

"You doubt my prison's security?" scowled the Commander, offended. "Absolutely not," Zeng replied, quaking with fear. "Shifu does. I'm just the messenger."

The Commander took Zeng on a tour of the prison, stopping at a bridge to show that an escape was impossible. "Whoah," said Zeng, peering into the cavernous space below. The Commander gave him a pat on the back, releasing a feather that drifted downwards. "One way in, one way out, one thousand guards and one prisoner," said the rhino. "Yes, except that prisoner is Tai Lung..." Zeng pointed out.

Having gone down in the lift, Zeng was taken through door after door before reaching a drawbridge that led to an island when lowered. "Behold Tai Lung," said the Commander. Zeng really didn't feel the need to get close to the legendary prisoner.

"I'll um... I'm just gonna wait right here," he stuttered, but the Commander pushed him forward. "It's perfectly safe," he assured him, before ordering the guards to have their crossbows ready. "Crossbows?" gulped Zeng. He crept towards the huge, muscular snow leopard that was bound, motionless, in a giant piece of tortoiseshell armour and chains. The Commander strode up to his prisoner and to Zeng's horror told him the news. "Hey, tough guy. Oogway's finally giving someone the Dragon Scroll and it's not gonna be you!"

"What are you doing?" asked Zeng
incredulously. "Don't get him mad!"
The Commander insisted that Tai Lung could
not move and stood on his tail to prove it.
"Aw. Did I step on the witty
kitty's tail?" he mocked.
Tai Lung stayed still, his eyes
staring coldly ahead.
"I'm good," said Zeng. "I've
seen enough. I'll tell Shifu he's
got nothing to worry about."
As they hurried back to the
lift, Zeng's feather fluttered
slowly to and fro behind
them until it landed in
front of Tai Lung. As
quick as a flash, he
grabbed it with his tail.

Meanwhile, the new Dragon Warrior found himself in the sacred Hall of Warriors. "Whoa. Would you look at this place!" gasped Po, peering at all the ancient kung fu artefacts. "The legendary Urn of Whispering Warriors! Said to contain the souls of the entire Tenshu Army... helloooo?" Shifu silently entered the hall in time to see the panda calling into the urn. "Have you finished sight-seeing?" he asked sternly. Po gasped, thinking the voice had come from the urn. "Sorry," he said to it. "I should've come to see you first." "My patience is wearing thin," warned Shifu. Po was puzzled. It's not like the urn was going anywhere! When he was told to turn round, he obeyed. "Master Shifu!" he exclaimed with a start, knocking the urn to the floor so that it smashed. "Someone... broke that," he added. "I'll fix it. Do you have some glue?"

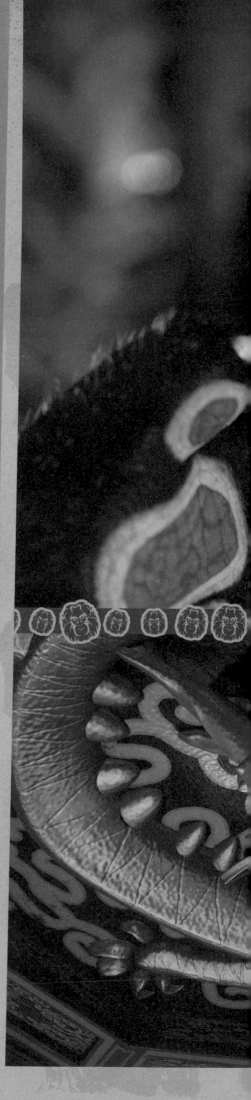

Po fumbled around, trying to pick up the urn pieces.
"Ow! Ooh. Splinter," he winced.
"So you're the legendary Dragon Warrior, hmm?" said
Shifu, not impressed.
"Uh... I guess so?" replied Po uncertainly.
"Wrong!" the master corrected him. "You will never be
the Dragon Warrior until you have learnt the secret of the
Dragon Scroll."
He pointed to an elaborately carved dragon on the ceiling.
"Whoa," said Po, seeing the scroll in its mouth. It was
way out of reach. "So how does this work? You have a
ladder or a trampoline or...?"
"You think it's that easy?" snapped Shifu. "That I am just
going to hand you the secret to limitless power? One must
first master the highest level of kung fu. And that is clearly
impossible if that one is someone like you."

"Someone like me?" asked Po.

"Yes," said Shifu, walking around the panda with his staff to point out his weaknesses. "Look at you – fat butt, flabby arms, ridiculous belly... and utter disregard for personal hygiene. I can smell your breath."

"Now wait a minute," Po objected, pointing at Shifu. "That's a little uncalled for. Oogway said that I was the..." He gasped as Shifu held his outstretched finger in a powerful grip. "The Wuxi finger hold?" he squeaked. "Not the Wuxi finger hold!"

"Oh, you know this hold?" the master asked slyly.

"DevelopedbyMasterWuxiintheThirdDynasty yes!" came the garbled reply.

"Oh, then you know what happens when I flex my pinky?"

"No no no!" Po nodded quickly. When Shifu said the hardest part was cleaning up afterwards, Po was ready to do anything he said.

"Listen, panda," said Shifu. "Oogway may have picked you, but when I'm through with you, you're going to wish he hadn't. Are we clear?"
"Yeah, we're clear," agreed Po. "We are so clear."

Still nursing his wounded finger, Po followed his master to the training hall. He stood and gawped as the Five effortlessly performed death-defying kung fu moves. "I – I don't know if I can do all those moves,"

As Po prepared to do a move on the dummy, the Five gathered round him curiously.

"Um, are they gonna watch?" asked Po. "Or should I wait until they get back to work or something?"

"Hit it," ordered Shifu.

"Okay. I mean, I just ate," Po tried another excuse. "So my kung fu might not be as good as later on."

Po psyched himself up and astonished the others by bouncing around, shuffling his feet and flapping his arms.

"Get ready to feel the thunder," he burbled. "I'm comin' at him with the crazy feet. I'm a blur, I'm a blur. You never seen bear style, you only seen praying Mantis."

"Would you hit it?" Shifu interrupted impatiently. Po tapped the dummy and it rocked back into place, so he was told to hit it harder.

stammered Po. "Maybe we could find something more suited to my level."

"And what level is that?" asked Shifu.

"Well, uh, let's just start at level zero." Unfortunately for Po, there was no such thing. "Hey! Maybe I could start with that?" he suggested, pointing to a friendly-looking dummy.

"That's for training children" scoffed Shifu. "And for propping the door open when it's hot. But if you insist..."

41

Po knocked it all the way backwards the second time and was quite proud of himself. "How's tha..." he began, before WHAP! The dummy sprang back and sent him flying. Totally dazed, he stumbled his way through the equipment, watched by the bemused Five. "This'll be easier than I thought," mused Shifu, as a swinging spiked ball swept Po into the Jade Tortoise of Wisdom. The panda was rocked around until he felt sick and rolled out towards the Gauntlet of Wooden Warriors. "Ow! These are hard," he complained, taking a pummelling from them before emerging on a part of floor that had bursts of flame leaping from it: the Field of Fiery Death. "How did I do?" asked Po eventually, battered, bruised and singed by his task. "There is now a level zero," Shifu replied.

"I don't understand what Master Oogway was thinking," said Viper, as the Five made their way to the bunkhouse that night. "The poor guy's just gonna get himself killed."
"He is so mighty!" Crane impersonated the old master. "The Dragon Warrior fell out of the sky on a ball of fire!"
"One would think that Master Oogway would choose someone who actually knew kung fu," scoffed Tigress.
"Or could at least touch his toes," said Crane.
"Or even see his toes," added Monkey.
None of them had noticed Po a few steps behind. He lifted up his belly to try and see his toes, but had to lean so far forward that he fell right over. He got up and gazed after the Five, letting out a big sigh.

TURN TO PAGE 52 TO SEE HOW PO SETTLES INTO LIFE AT THE JADE PALACE!

TRAINING TIME

ONCE SHIFU HAS FINISHED DEMONSTRATING THE WUXI FINGER HOLD ON PO, HE WILL TAKE HIM FOR A TOUGH TRAINING SESSION WITH THE FIVE. WHICH WAY SHOULD THEY GO TO GET TO THE TRAINING HALL?

START

FINISH

FORTUNE STICKS

SHIFU HAS A FUN WAY FOR YOU AND YOUR FRIENDS TO TELL YOUR FORTUNE! ALL YOU NEED TO DO IS THROW TWO DICE TOGETHER AND SEE WHAT THEY ADD UP TO. THEN LOOK AT THE FORTUNE STICK WITH THE SAME NUMBER ON IT TO SEE WHAT THERE IS IN STORE FOR YOU. REMEMBER, IT'S JUST FOR FUN SO YOU CAN THROW AS MANY TIMES AS YOU LIKE!

2. If your dice add up to two, a friend has some good news for you.

3. The dice are showing two and one, a trip this week will be great fun!

4. You have thrown the number four, a gift will soon come through your door.

5. If your number's five today, an invitation is on its way.

6. If your dice add up to six, beware of close friends playing tricks!

7. This number brings most luck, they say; it's good for you in every way.

8. The number eight brings out your best, you will do well in your next test.

9. A number nine brings something funny, as well as extra pocket money.

10. A ten brings luck to those who play, your team is sure to win today.

11. This odd number's good for you, so make a wish – it could come true!

12. Your two dice are showing double... the colour purple could bring trouble!

MAKE A CHINESE LANTERN

PAPER LANTERNS ARE TRADITIONALLY MADE AT THE END OF THE CHINESE NEW YEAR CELEBRATIONS, BUT THEY LOOK SO GOOD THAT YOU CAN MAKE ONE ANY TIME!

FOR EACH LANTERN YOU WILL NEED:

- A sheet of white or coloured paper, about A4 size
- Round-ended scissors
- Sticky tape

1. First cut a 2 cm strip from the short end of your paper. This will be the handle for your lantern.

2. Fold the rest of the paper in half lengthways and draw a line along the long open edge of your paper, 2 cm from the edge. This will be the line where you stop cutting.

3. Draw straight lines about 2 cm apart from the folded edge towards the open edge, stopping at the first line that you drew.

4. Cut along the lines from the folded edge and open out your paper.

5. Make a lantern shape by joining the short edges together with tape.

6. Tape on the handle and you have your lantern!

YOU CAN USE PENS, PAINT AND GLITTER TO DECORATE YOUR LANTERN. IF YOU MAKE SEVERAL, YOU CAN THREAD THEM ONTO STRING OR RIBBON AND HANG THEM UP!

PO'S PICTURE PUZZLE

PO WILL HAVE TO WORK REALLY HARD IF HE WANTS TO BE ACCEPTED BY THE FIVE! WHAT WILL HE BE DOING DURING HIS STAY AT THE JADE PALACE? TO FIND OUT, SEE HOW MANY LETTERS SPELL OUT EACH OF THE PICTURE CLUES AND THEN WRITE THEM IN TO THE CORRECT BOXES. THE ANSWERS ARE AT THE BACK OF YOUR ANNUAL.

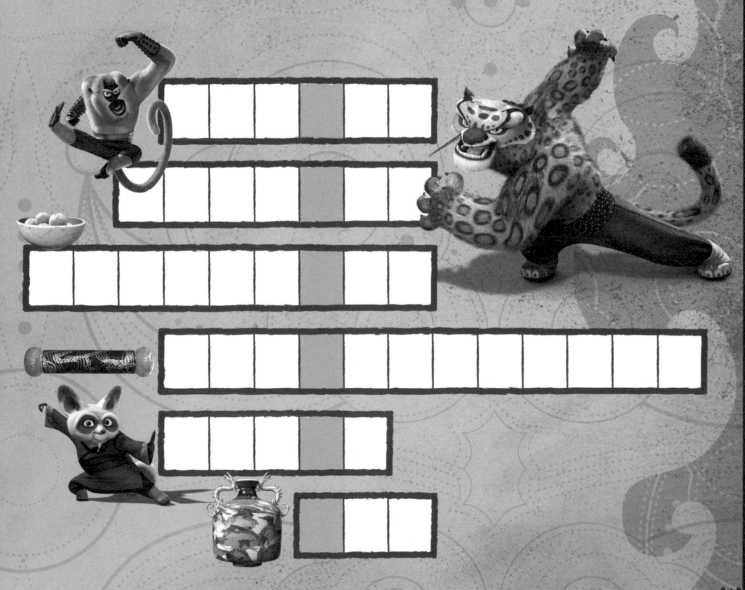

READY FOR BATTLE

THE FURIOUS FIVE ARE USED TO WOWING AUDIENCES WITH THEIR INCREDIBLE MARTIAL ARTS SKILLS. LOOK AT THESE TWO PICTURES OF THE GROUP PREPARING TO FIGHT IN THE PALACE ARENA AND SEE IF YOU CAN SPOT THE TEN DIFFERENCES BETWEEN THEM.

MATCH PAIRS PUZZLE

LOOK CAREFULLY AT THESE PICTURES OF PO AND HIS KUNG FU FRIENDS. WHO IS ABOVE MONKEY, BELOW TIGRESS AND BETWEEN VIPER AND PO? THE ANSWER IS AT THE BACK OF YOUR ANNUAL.

ALPHABET NOODLE

PO IS FINALLY FIGHTING ALONGSIDE HIS IDOLS... EVEN IF THEY'RE NOT EXACTLY HAPPY ABOUT IT! SEE IF YOU CAN FIND EACH OF THE FURIOUS FIVE'S NAMES IN THE NOODLE BELOW AND THEN SPELL OUT AN ANCIENT MASTER'S NAME WITH THE LETTERS THAT ARE LEFT OVER.

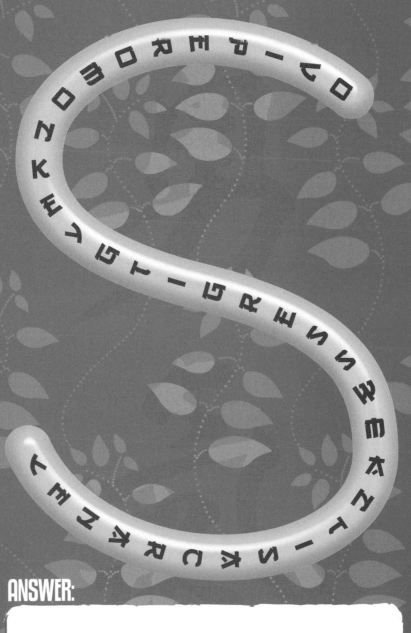

ANSWER:

TOMORROW IS A MISTERY

Po crept into the bunkhouse, trying not to draw attention to himself. He tiptoed across the hall as lightly as he could, but the straining floorboards creaked loudly at his feet. "Great," he whispered. He was determined that his next step would be as silent as a ninja's. CRACK! His foot went right through the floor. As he struggled to keep his balance, Po made still more noise and ended up falling through Crane's bedroom door.

"Hi... you're up," Po ventured. "Am now," said Crane flatly. "Some day, huh?" Po tried to make more conversation. "That kung fu stuff is hard work, right? Your biceps sore?"

Crane glanced at his wing, but decided not to take it further.

"Um, I've had a long and rather disappointing day, so... yeah, I should probably get to sleep now," he pointed out.

Po agreed, but couldn't quite bring himself
to leave the room.
"It's just... I'm such a big fan," he told
Crane. "You guys were totally amazing
at the Battle of Weeping River.
Outnumbered a thousand to one, but
you didn't stop and then you just HI-YAH!"
Po jerked his body around in a series of
clumsy kung fu moves until RI-I-IP! He put his
foot through the screen wall.
"Oo, sorry about that," he winced.
"Look, you don't belong here," said Crane.
"I know, I know. You're right," Po agreed sadly.
"I just... my whole life I've dreamed of..."
"No, I meant you don't belong in this room.
This is my room, property of Crane."
"Right, right. I'm keeping you up. We got big
things tomorrow," gabbled the star-struck
panda. "You're awesome. Last thing I'm
gonna say. Bye."

Po tiptoed down past more rooms. Creak, creak. Tigress opened her door.

"Hey, Tigress. Didn't mean to wake you. Just, uh..."

"You don't belong here," Tigress interrupted.

"Yeah, yeah," Po nodded. "This is your room."

"I mean you don't belong in the Jade Palace," she said bluntly. "You're a disgrace to kung fu and if you have any respect for who we are and what we do, you will be gone by morning." Po had no time to reply before Tigress shut the door.

"Big fan..." he said anyway. He decided to go for a walk.

"I see you have found the Sacred Peach Tree of Heavenly Wisdom," said Master Oogway, who had been looking for Po.

"Is that what this is?" gasped Po.

Po's mouth was full of peach and juice was dripping from his chin. "I am so sorry. I thought it was just a regular peach tree."

"I understand," said Oogway. "You eat when you are upset."

Po insisted that he wasn't upset, but soon realised that it was obvious.

"I probably sucked more today than anyone in the history of kung fu," he explained, "in the history of China, in the history of sucking."

"Probably," nodded Oogway.

"How's Shifu ever going to turn me into the Dragon Warrior? I'm not like the Five. I've got no claws, no wings, no venom. Even Mantis has those... thingies. Maybe I should just quit and go back to making noodles."

"Quit, don't quit," shrugged Oogway. "Noodles, don't noodles."

Po looked confused.

"You are too concerned with what was and what will be," said Oogway. "There is a saying: yesterday is history, tomorrow is a mystery, but today is a gift. That is why it is called the present."

As he walked away, he tapped the tree with his staff and a peach fell into Po's hand.

Up in the frozen mountain, Tai Lung had put Zeng's feather to good use and picked the lock so he could burst free from his armour.

"What's happening?" gasped Zeng, as alarms sounded around him. Seeing that only shackles now tethered the powerful leopard, Commander Vachir ordered the crossbows to be fired. Tai Lung nimbly used the spears to break loose and then kicked them back into the walls to make a staircase.

"Tai Lung is free!" cried Zeng. "I must warn Shifu!"

"You're not going anywhere," growled the Commander, holding on to the panic-stricken goose. "And neither is he." He ordered the lift to be brought up but Tai Lung caught it, dodging the shower of arrows being fired at him. The guards cut the rope so that the lift crashed to the ground, but still the leopard sprang ever higher. He leaped onto a bridge above, fighting his way through the guards

to get to the level where the Commander stood watching the disaster unfold.
"We are so very, very dead," whimpered Zeng. "Not yet we're not," grinned the Commander. "Now!"
As ordered, the archers set off charges on the ceiling, sending huge stalactites crashing down into the prison.

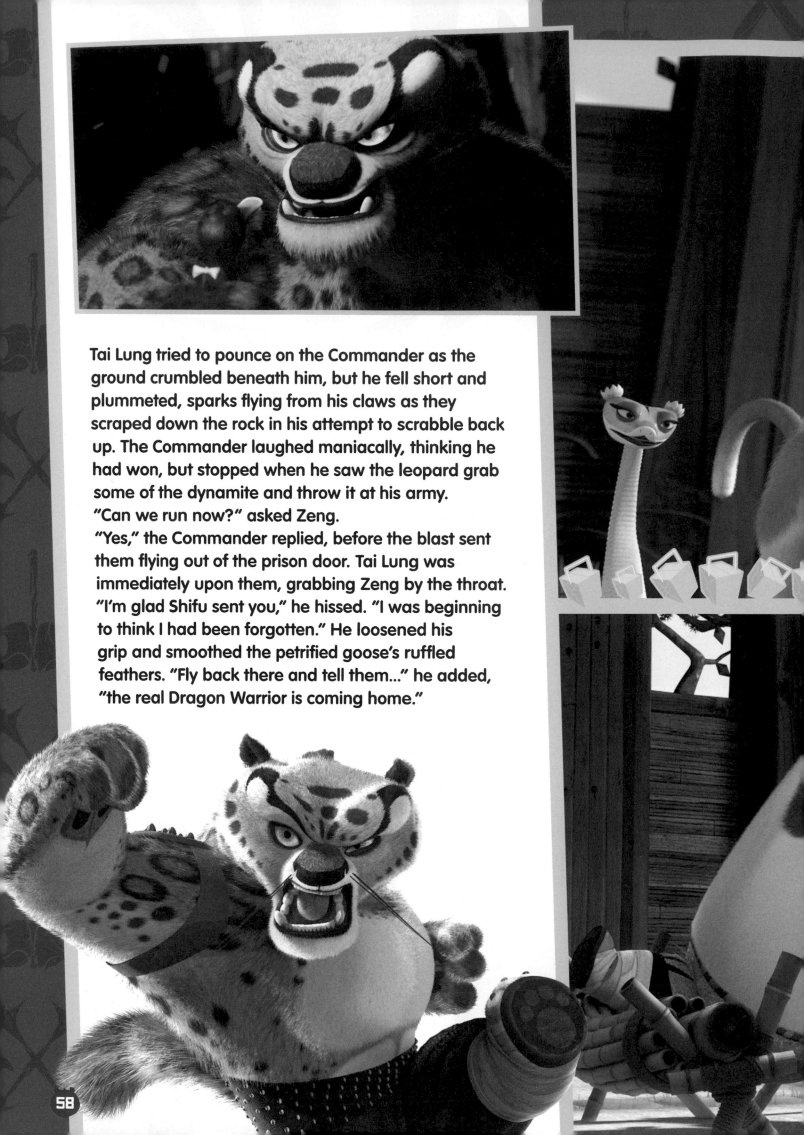

Tai Lung tried to pounce on the Commander as the ground crumbled beneath him, but he fell short and plummeted, sparks flying from his claws as they scraped down the rock in his attempt to scrabble back up. The Commander laughed maniacally, thinking he had won, but stopped when he saw the leopard grab some of the dynamite and throw it at his army. "Can we run now?" asked Zeng.

"Yes," the Commander replied, before the blast sent them flying out of the prison door. Tai Lung was immediately upon them, grabbing Zeng by the throat. "I'm glad Shifu sent you," he hissed. "I was beginning to think I had been forgotten." He loosened his grip and smoothed the petrified goose's ruffled feathers. "Fly back there and tell them..." he added, "the real Dragon Warrior is coming home."

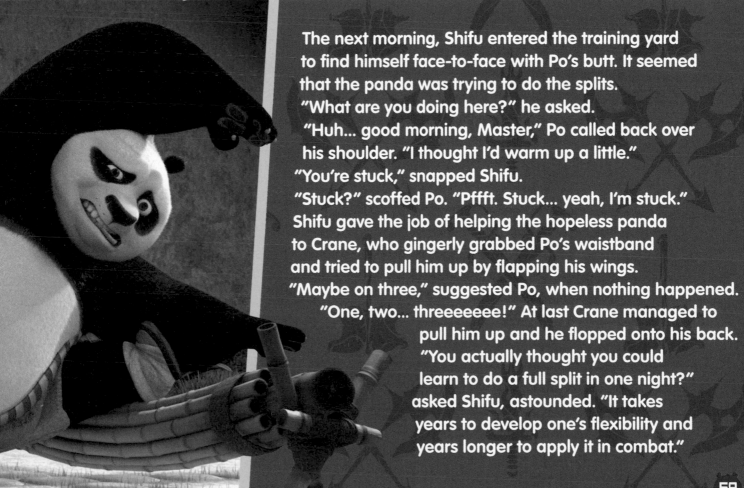

The next morning, Shifu entered the training yard to find himself face-to-face with Po's butt. It seemed that the panda was trying to do the splits.

"What are you doing here?" he asked.

"Huh... good morning, Master," Po called back over his shoulder. "I thought I'd warm up a little."

"You're stuck," snapped Shifu.

"Stuck?" scoffed Po. "Pffft. Stuck... yeah, I'm stuck."

Shifu gave the job of helping the hopeless panda to Crane, who gingerly grabbed Po's waistband and tried to pull him up by flapping his wings.

"Maybe on three," suggested Po, when nothing happened. "One, two... threeeeeee!" At last Crane managed to pull him up and he flopped onto his back.

"You actually thought you could learn to do a full split in one night?" asked Shifu, astounded. "It takes years to develop one's flexibility and years longer to apply it in combat."

To show what a true master was capable of, Shifu flung two boards into the air. Tigress leaped up and did a perfect split kick, smashing them to pieces that landed around Po. Awestruck, he picked a piece up as a souvenir. "Put that down!" scolded Shifu. "The only souvenirs we collect here are bloody knuckles and broken bones. Let's get started." He chose Viper to be Po's first opponent.

Po was proving to be worse than useless. When he tried to spar with Crane on the rim of the Jade Tortoise, he fell in and was again rocked around until he felt sick. In fact, he spent the whole day being beaten, falling on his face time after time.

"I've been taking it easy on you, panda," Shifu told him, "but no more! Your next opponent will be me."

"All right!" said Po excitedly. "Let's go!"

The Five exchanged worried looks as their master told him to step forth and briskly whirled him round, throwing him to the floor and pinning back his arm.

"The true path to victory is to find your opponent's weakness and make him suffer for it," Shifu explained, whipping Po round again. "To take his strength and use it against him until he finally falls, or quits."

Shifu paused, holding Po by the nose.

"But a real warrior never quits," said Po. "Don't worry, Master. I will never quit!"

Shifu flung Po upwards in frustration and leaped at him with a flying kick.

"Are you ready?" she asked. "I was born ready," joked Po, but before he knew what was happening, she had hurled him into the air. "I'm sorry, brother," cooed Viper to Po, who had landed on his head. "I thought you said you were ready." "That was awesome!" Po exclaimed. "Let's go again!" Shifu then watched in exasperation as Monkey used a staff on Po, meeting no resistance whatsoever.

Later, after the hard day's training, Mantis offered to give Po a little acupuncture. "Aaaoo... eeeee," Po grimaced. "I thought you said this would make me feel better."

"Trust me, it will," said Mantis, sticking more needles in. "It's just not easy finding the right nerve points under all this..."

"Fat?" Po finished the sentence for him.

"Fur," insisted Mantis. "I was gonna say fur. Who am I to judge a warrior by his size? I mean, look at me." Po tried, but the insect was hopping about all over the place, putting in more needles.

"Maybe you should look at this again," Viper suggested, holding up a diagram of acupuncture meridians that had a panda sketched over it.

"Oh. Okay," agreed Mantis.

"Yow!" Po yelped again. "If I didn't know any better," he added, trying to hold a normal conversation, "I'd say Master Shifu was trying to get rid of me."

The others laughed awkwardly.

"I know he can seem heartless," said Mantis. "But he wasn't always like that."

"According to legend, there was a time when Master Shifu used to smile," added Viper. "But that was before..."

"Before what?" asked Po, fascinated.

"Before Tai Lung," answered Tigress. Crane reminded her that they weren't really supposed to talk about him, but she decided that Po should know. "Shifu found him as a cub and raised him as a son," she began.

"When the boy showed talent in kung fu, Shifu trained him. He believed in him, telling him he was destined for greatness."
Po listened intently. He had heard of Tai Lung and knew he was in prison, but this was the first time he had been told the full story.
"It was never enough for Tai Lung," Tigress continued. "He wanted the Dragon Scroll, but Oogway saw darkness in his heart and refused. Outraged, Tai Lung laid waste to the valley. He tried to take the scroll by force and Shifu had to destroy what he had created. But how could he? Shifu loved Tai Lung like he'd never loved anyone before... or since."
Tigress fell silent as she dwelled on how hard she'd worked over the years to get just a little praise from Master Shifu.

IS THIS THE END OF THE DRAGON WARRIOR? FIND OUT ON PAGE 72!

Whatever Tigress had done, it had always fallen short of Shifu's expectations. But the Dragon Scroll was still waiting; Master Oogway had battled with Tai Lung to protect it. Tigress felt anger welling up inside her as she remembered how close she herself had come to holding the Dragon Scroll. "Now he has a chance to make things right, to train the true Dragon Warrior, and he's stuck with you: a big, fat panda who treats it like a joke."

"Doieeee..." gurgled Po, making a googly-eyed face. "Oh, that is it!" she cried, lunging at him.

"Wait!" Mantis stopped her. "My fault! I accidentally tweaked his facial nerve." Po fell forwards, revealing his needle-covered back.

"And I may have also stopped his heart," he added.

WARRIOR WORDSEARCH

WHILE PO RECOVERS FROM HIS ACUPUNCTURE SESSION, LOOK AT THIS WORDSEARCH SQUARE AND SEE IF YOU CAN FIND ALL THE KUNG FU PANDA WORDS AND CHARACTERS LISTED. THE WORDS READ UP, DOWN, BACKWARDS, FORWARDS AND DIAGONALLY.

D	R	A	G	O	N	W	A	R	R	I	O	R	E
R	B	G	Q	M	A	N	T	I	S	Z	E	G	C
A	E	N	O	O	D	L	E	S	R	P	J	N	A
G	N	I	P	R	M	W	R	E	I	R	A	V	E
O	A	L	Y	C	H	A	Z	V	S	E	D	T	P
N	R	P	E	G	N	U	L	I	A	T	E	I	F
S	C	M	K	K	U	N	G	F	U	S	P	G	O
C	B	U	N	K	H	O	U	S	E	A	A	R	Y
R	Z	D	O	Q	T	N	Y	U	Z	M	L	E	E
O	K	E	M	G	Y	A	P	O	W	Z	A	S	L
L	C	I	N	E	W	S	H	I	F	U	C	S	L
L	A	Z	J	G	N	B	P	R	Y	H	E	T	A
B	J	M	O	L	L	Y	O	U	W	U	X	I	V
S	R	O	I	R	R	A	W	F	O	L	L	A	H

- KUNG FU
- MASTER
- SHIFU
- TIGRESS
- VIPER
- MONKEY
- MANTIS
- CRANE
- OOGWAY
- BUNKHOUSE
- MR PING
- ZENG
- TAI LUNG
- FURIOUS FIVE
- JADE PALACE
- DRAGON WARRIOR
- VALLEY OF PEACE
- NOODLES
- DRAGON SCROLL
- DUMPLING
- HALL OF WARRIORS
- WUXI

MAKE A MASK

YOU AND YOUR FRIENDS CAN BE KUNG FU PANDA FOR A DAY! TO MAKE PO MASKS YOU'LL NEED:

- Thin Card (Such As A Cereal Box)
- Safe Glue
- Round-ended Scissors
- Thin elastic Band

ALL YOU NEED TO DO FOR EACH MASK IS:

1. Ask a grown-up to copy this page.
2. Stick your page onto the thin card.
3. Cut around the mask and ask your grown-up to cut out holes for the eyes and the ends of elastic.
4. Tie each end of the elastic to your mask and put it on. HI-YAH!

WHAT'S YOUR YEAR?

The Chinese calendar is different from ours in that it is based on the movement of the moon around the Earth, rather than the movement of the Earth around the sun. Po and his friends celebrate New Year in January or February, depending on when the new moon is.

Chinese years go in a cycle of twelve, with each year being named after an animal – 2009 is the Year of the Ox. If you were born in the year 2000, for example, you were born in the year of the Dragon and you might have a dragon's characteristics. See which Chinese year you were born in and find out if you are anything like its animal. Then do the same for your friends and relatives!

YEARS OF THE RAT:

1960 :: 1972 :: 1984 :: 1996 :: 2008

Rats are clever and work hard. They have a good imagination and although they may not always plan ahead, they are devoted and loyal.

YEARS OF THE TIGER:

1950 :: 1962 :: 1974 :: 1986 :: 1998

Tigress is adventurous and isn't afraid to take risks. Like all Tigers, she has a cool exterior to some but is warm and generous to those close to her.

YEARS OF THE OX:

1961 :: 1973 :: 1985 :: 1997 :: 2009

People born in the Year of the Ox are well organised and often make good leaders. They have lots of patience and know their own mind.

YEARS OF THE RABBIT:

1951 :: 1963 :: 1975 :: 1987 :: 1999

Being gentle and affectionate, Rabbits are natural peacemakers. They are popular and fun-loving with strong family ties.

YEARS OF THE DRAGON:

1952 :: 1964 :: 1976 :: 1988 :: 2000

Believed to be the luckiest of all the animals, Dragons are lively and ambitious. They love to try new things and are an inspiration to others.

YEARS OF THE SNAKE:

1953 :: 1965 :: 1977 :: 1989 :: 2001

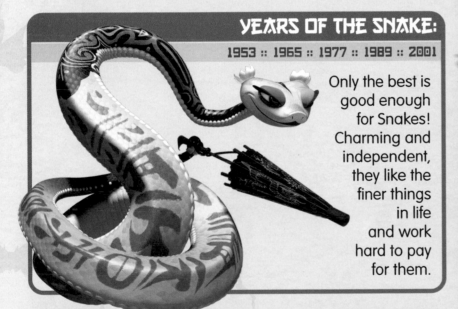

Only the best is good enough for Snakes! Charming and independent, they like the finer things in life and work hard to pay for them.

YEARS OF THE HORSE:

1954 :: 1966 :: 1978 :: 1990 :: 2002

Horses are intelligent and ambitious, enjoying success in whatever they do. They're good at multi-tasking and will never leave a job unfinished.

YEARS OF THE RAM:

1955 :: 1967 :: 1979 :: 1991 :: 2003

The most artistic of the animals, Rams are good-natured and avoid conflict. Although they are gentle, they have great inner strength.

YEARS OF THE MONKEY:

1956 :: 1968 :: 1980 :: 1992 :: 2004

Monkey is mischievous and loves a challenge! Others born in the Year of the Monkey are good problem solvers and are well liked.

YEARS OF THE ROOSTER:

1957 :: 1969 :: 1981 :: 1993 :: 2005

Roosters love to be the centre of attention. They are natural entertainers but may find fault with others... even if they don't like being criticised themselves!

YEARS OF THE DOG:

1958 :: 1970 :: 1982 :: 1994 :: 2006

Dogs are good listeners and are highly respected by others. They are honest and trustworthy but tend to worry too much.

YEARS OF THE PIG:

1959 :: 1971 :: 1983 :: 1995 :: 2007

Pigs are easy-going and generous, although they can be untidy to live with! They love to help others and always see the upside of any situation.

LEOPARD ON THE LOOSE

WHOAH! TAI LUNG IS FREE AND HE'S OUT TO FINISH THE BATTLE THAT HE STARTED WITH SHIFU TWENTY YEARS AGO! USE YOUR PENS OR PENCILS TO COLOUR HIM IN.

KUNG FU FIGHTING STYLES

A WARRIOR'S FIGHTING STYLE DEPENDS ON WHAT ANIMAL HE OR SHE IDENTIFIES WITH. TAKE A LOOK AT THESE TO DECIDE WHICH ONE YOU WOULD CHOOSE!

TIGRESS

Tiger-style kung fu is powerful, quick and aggressive. Tigress strikes directly without hesitation, shattering her opponent's defences. She is agile and stays close to the ground, fighting honourably without using her claws (unlike Tai Lung!)

MONKEY

Monkeys are acrobatic and a little comical. They use a surprise element, striking unpredictably from any position with rapid blows that seem to come from everywhere, all at once. Unlike the rest of the Five, Monkey also likes to use a staff.

VIPER

The traditional snake style is fluid and explosive. Viper's ability to contort her body into any shape makes her almost impossible to hit. She uses her lightning-fast reflexes to dodge blows before counter striking with deadly efficiency.

CRANE

Crane-style kung fu is graceful, effortless and balanced, with the fighter posing his striking hand to look like the long beak of a bird. Crane's wide wingspan allows him to deflect blows easily and stay balanced on the narrowest of surfaces.

MANTIS

Traditional Mantis-style moves are quick and precise. Mantis's small size and incredible speed make him virtually invisible to opponents, allowing him to leap on his powerful rear legs and strike unexpectedly.

TAI LUNG

Leopard-style fighting demands enormous upper body strength and speed. Tai Lung is a cunning master, quickly pinpointing his opponent's weakness and exploiting it. He is a brutal warrior who fights to win, even if it means breaking rules... and bones!

FAREWELL, OOGWAY

That evening, Shifu tried to meditate in the training hall. "Inner peace, inner peace, inner peace," he said, fidgeting. His concentration was then broken by the sound of wings flapping. "Oh, Zeng," he greeted his messenger. "Excellent. I could use some good news right now."

Minutes later, Shifu burst through the mist that swirled around the Peach Tree of Heavenly Wisdom. "Master!" he cried. "It's very bad news." "Ah, Shifu," Oogway remained calm. "There

"Master, that panda is not the Dragon Warrior," protested Shifu. "He wasn't even meant to be here. It was an accident!"

"There are no accidents," Oogway reminded him. "My old friend, the panda will never fulfil his destiny, nor you yours, until you let go of the illusion of control."

"Illusion?"

Oogway turned to the peach tree to explain what he meant.

"I cannot make this tree blossom when it suits me, nor make it bear fruit before its time."

"But there are things we can control," said Shifu, kicking the tree to make a peach fall at his feet. "I can control when the fruit will fall." A second peach then landed on his head, making Oogway chuckle. Shifu tossed it in the air and leaped up to split it with a chop, punching a hole in the ground for the stone to fall into.

is just news. There is no good or bad."

"Master, your vision was right," Shifu explained. "Tai Lung has broken out of prison. He's on his way!"

"That is bad news..." agreed the old master, "...if you do not believe that the Dragon Warrior can stop him."

"I can control where to plant the seed," he added.

"But no matter what you do," said Oogway, "that seed will grow to be a peach tree. You may wish for an apple or an orange, but you will get a peach." Shifu was losing his patience.

"But a peach cannot defeat Tai Lung!" he exclaimed.

"Maybe it can," smiled Oogway. "If you are willing to guide it, to nurture it. To believe in it. Promise me, Shifu, that you will believe."

"I... I will try," agreed Shifu, a little puzzled.

"Good. My time has come," Oogway announced. "You must continue your journey without me."

"What... what are you...?" stammered Shifu, as Oogway handed over his staff and backed away into the mist.

"Master, you can't leave me!"

"You must believe," echoed the voice for the last time. Oogway was gone forever.

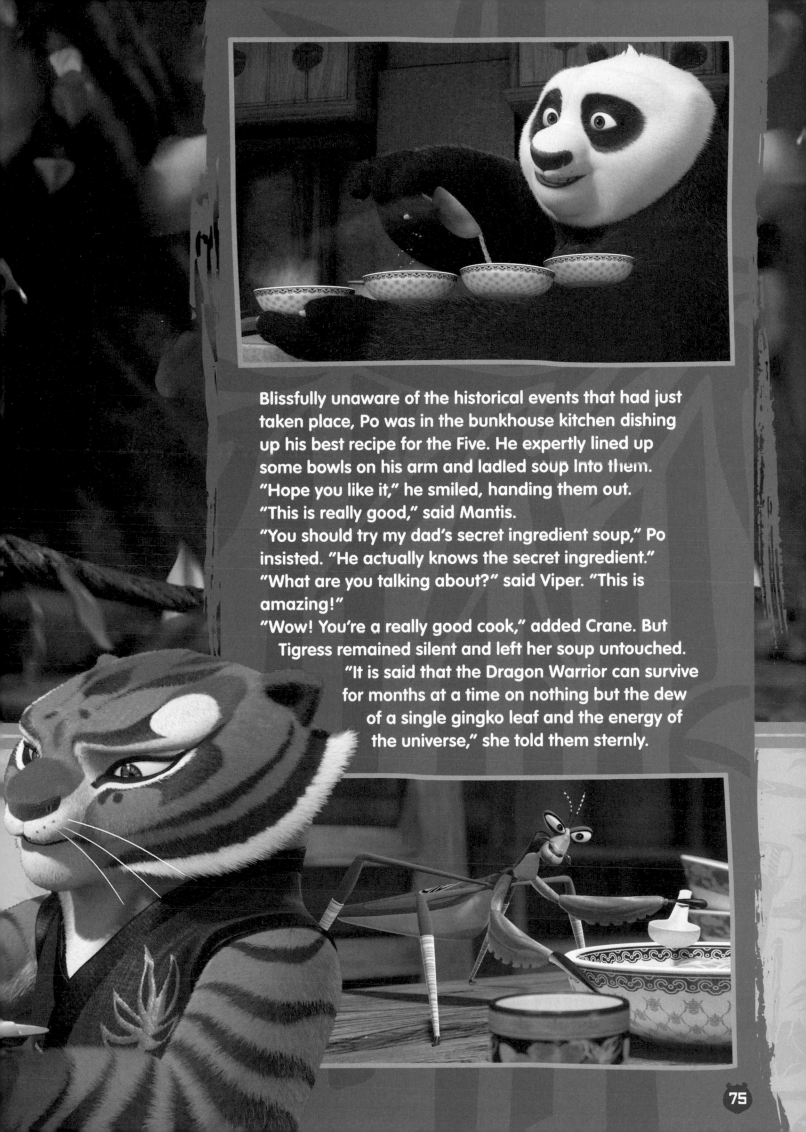

Blissfully unaware of the historical events that had just taken place, Po was in the bunkhouse kitchen dishing up his best recipe for the Five. He expertly lined up some bowls on his arm and ladled soup Into them. "Hope you like it," he smiled, handing them out. "This is really good," said Mantis.
"You should try my dad's secret ingredient soup," Po insisted. "He actually knows the secret ingredient."
"What are you talking about?" said Viper. "This is amazing!"
"Wow! You're a really good cook," added Crane. But Tigress remained silent and left her soup untouched.
"It is said that the Dragon Warrior can survive for months at a time on nothing but the dew of a single gingko leaf and the energy of the universe," she told them sternly.

The rest of the Five were lost for words. "I guess my body doesn't know it's the Dragon Warrior yet," Po shrugged. "I'm gonna need a lot more than dew and, uh, universe juice."
He picked up his bowl and took a big gulp of secret ingredient soup, then wondered why Mantis was giggling. "What?" he asked.
"Oh, nothing," replied Mantis, "Master Shifu!" The others laughed as Po realised he had a noodle moustache.
"You will never be the Dragon Warrior unless you lose five hundred pounds and brush your teeth!" chuckled Po, as he impersonated his master. "What is that noise you're making? Laughter? I've never heard of it!" He grabbed two empty bowls and held them up to make ears. "Work hard, panda, and maybe some day you will have ears like mine."

As the others enjoyed Po's performance, Tigress leaned forward to sniff the soup, but then looked up and froze. The laughter suddenly stopped.
"It's Shifu," hissed Monkey.
"Of course it's Shifu," chuckled Po, oblivious to the master behind him. "What do you think I'm doing?"
"You think this is funny?" snapped Shifu. "Tai Lung has escaped and you're acting like children! He is

coming for the Dragon Scroll," he turned to Po, "and you are the only one who can stop him." Po could only laugh, thinking the master had finally found his sense of humour and was winding him up. But Shifu's expression was grave.

"Um, Master Oogway will stop him," Po said, beginning to panic. "He did it before, he'll do it again!"

"Oogway cannot," Shifu told them sadly. "Not anymore." Only then did the Five notice that their master was holding Oogway's staff and realised its significance.

"Our only hope is the Dragon Warrior," added Shifu.

"Master, let us stop Tai Lung," said Tigress. "This is what you've trained us for."

"No. It is not your destiny to defeat Tai Lung. It is his." Shifu pointed at Po... but he had vanished.

"How am I supposed to beat Tai Lung?" Po asked. "I can't even beat you to the steps."

"You will beat him because you are the Dragon Warrior," Shifu answered, trying to convince himself as well as Po.

"You don't believe that," said Po. "From the moment I got here, you've been trying to get rid of me."

"Yes, I have," admitted Shifu. "But now I ask you to trust in your master as I have come to trust in mine."

"You're not my master. And I'm not the Dragon Warrior."

"Then why didn't you quit?"

"I stayed," Po explained, "because every time you threw a brick at my head or said I smelled, It hurt. But it could never hurt more than it did every day of my life just being me."

Po had decided to make a run for it. He raced from the bunkhouse, looking over his shoulder to check he wasn't being followed. "You cannot leave!" exclaimed Shifu, landing in front of him from nowhere. "A real warrior never quits!"

"Watch me," said Po. He tried to manoeuvre himself round Shifu, but it was impossible.

Po gazed down at the valley, his home, and turned back to Shifu.

"I thought if anyone could make me... not me, it was you. The greatest kung fu teacher in all of China."

"But I can change you!" Shifu insisted. "I can turn you into the Dragon Warrior!"

"Come on. Even if it takes Tai Lung a hundred years to get here, how are you gonna change this..." he pointed to his belly, "...into the Dragon Warrior? How?"

"I don't know!" yelled Shifu. Then, with a sigh, "I don't know." He moved out of Po's way to let him go.

Watching from a distance, Tigress suddenly sped off towards the mountains, followed closely by the other four. "Don't try and stop me," she warned them. But they weren't trying to stop her; they were going with her.

Early the next morning, Shifu went to investigate
noises coming from the bunkhouse and found Po
in the kitchen, stuffing food into his mouth.
"What?" asked Po, mid-munch. "I eat when I'm
upset, okay?"
"Oh, no need to explain," Shifu assured him, a glint in his
eye. "I just thought you might be Monkey. He hides his
cookies on the top shelf." After leaving the kitchen, Shifu hid
behind the doorway and waited to see if his suspicions
were correct. He was amazed to see Po nimbly climb
up the cupboards to reach the cookies and jam
them into his mouth. Smiling, he walked back in.
"Don't tell Monkey," Po mumbled, sending
a shower of crumbs from his mouth.
"Look at you," said Shifu. "How
did you get up there?"

Po wasn't entirely sure how he had reached the top of the cupboard; he was just getting some cookies.

"And yet you are ten feet off the ground and have done a perfect split," Shifu pointed out.

"No, this... this is just an accident."

As soon as Po was aware of what he was doing, WHUMP! He slipped to the floor.

Now it was Shifu's turn to say: "There are no accidents."

Po obligingly splashed water under his arms. "Panda, we do not wash our pits in the Pool of Sacred Tears," said Shifu. "This is where Oogway unravelled the mysteries of harmony and focus. This is the birthplace of kung fu."

Po looked in wonder at his surroundings. He was in a magical place.

"Do you want to learn kung fu?" asked Shifu.

"Yeah," Po replied.

"Then I am your master."

Po sniffed back tears of joy as he followed Shifu to a clearing.

"When you focus on kung fu, when you concentrate... you suck," the master told him. "But perhaps that is my fault. I cannot train you the way I have trained the Five. I now see that the way to get through to you is with this!" Po was delighted to see that 'this' was a bowl of dumplings.

Soon afterwards, Shifu was leading Po through the mountains.

"I know you're trying to be all mystical and kung fuey, but could you at least tell me where we're going?" asked Po. He got no answer. They walked and walked until at last they stopped by a turquoise pool.

"You dragged me all the way out here for a bath?" wheezed the exhausted panda.

Shifu promised that Po could eat after his training session. Once the panda had completed his breathing exercises, balance tests, press-ups, sit-ups and climbing, the bowl of dumplings was finally set before him.
"Just like that?" he asked suspiciously.
"You are free to eat," replied Shifu. "Enjoy."
Po took a dumpling in his chopsticks and raised it to his mouth when WHOOSH! Shifu snatched it away and ate it.

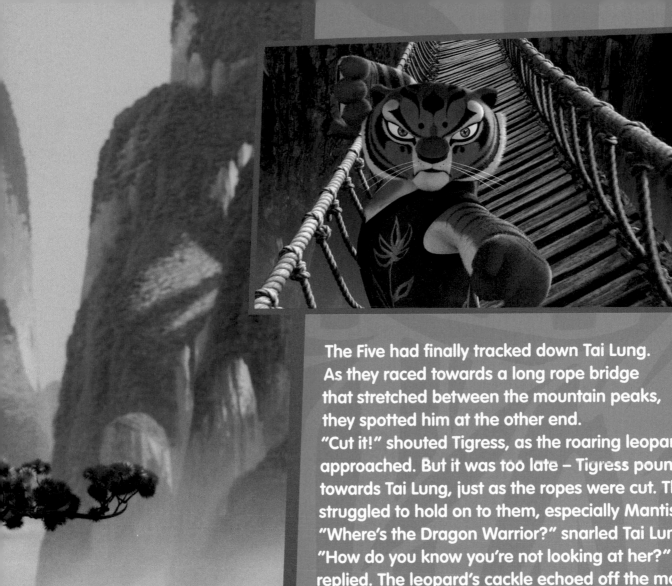

The Five had finally tracked down Tai Lung.
As they raced towards a long rope bridge
that stretched between the mountain peaks,
they spotted him at the other end.
"Cut it!" shouted Tigress, as the roaring leopard
approached. But it was too late – Tigress pounced
towards Tai Lung, just as the ropes were cut. The others
struggled to hold on to them, especially Mantis.
"Where's the Dragon Warrior?" snarled Tai Lung.
"How do you know you're not looking at her?" Tigress
replied. The leopard's cackle echoed off the mountains.
"You think I'm a fool?" he sneered. "I know you're
not the Dragon Warrior. None of you! I heard how
he fell out of the sky on a ball of fire, that he's
unlike any warrior the world has ever seen."
The Five exchanged worried looks.
He was right... in a way!

"Hey!" Po protested.
Realising that this was his
final challenge, Po slammed
the table and sent the
dumplings into the air. He
and Shifu sparred frantically
with their chopsticks until Po
outmanoeuvred Shifu for the
last one. But he didn't feel
hungry anymore; he was
filled with pride instead.
"I'm not hungry... Master,"
Po said, handing it over.
The teacher and his
pupil bowed respectfully
to one another.

SEE WHAT HAPPENS WHEN TAI LUNG MEETS
THE DRAGON WARRIOR ON PAGE 94!

CHOP CHOP!

PO IS A TRUE CHOPSTICK MASTER - HE CAN EVEN OUT-CHOPSTICK SHIFU! NOW IT'S YOUR TURN TO HAVE SOME CHOPSTICK FUN.

FRAME A FRIEND

Wooden chopsticks can be used to make a simple square or rectangular frame for a picture of your favourite warrior... or maybe your best friend! For each frame, you'll need:

- Four chopsticks (cut to size by a grown-up if required)
- Thin card
- Safe glue

ALL YOU NEED TO DO IS:

1. Stick your photo to the thin card and use round-ended scissors to cut around it, leaving a 1 cm border.

2. Stick one chopstick along a border and a second along the opposite side.

3. Complete the frame by sticking the other chopsticks onto the first two (at right angles).

DID YOU KNOW...?

Chopsticks have been used in China for more than 4000 years! (Not the same ones, obviously.)

Chopsticks are also used in Japan, Korea, Vietnam and Taiwan.

Early chopsticks were made from bamboo, jade, ivory or bone.

A tax was added to disposable chopsticks in China in 2006, as 45 billion pairs were being thrown away every year!

Emperors in ancient China had chopsticks made from silver... to detect any poison in their food! If the chopsticks turned black, the Emperor knew his food was dodgy.

Dropping your chopsticks is said to bring bad luck.

Forkchops are chopsticks at one end and a knife and fork at the other, just in case you need rescuing!

CHOPSTICK CHALLENGE

Look at this chopstick pile and see if you can count how many chopsticks there are altogether. The answer is at the back of your annual.

WRITE AWAY

How many words can you make from these letters? The first one is done for you – see if you can make it to twenty! Remember, plurals are allowed.

CHOPSTICKS

1. chips
2.
3.
4.
5.
6.
7.
8.
9.
10.
11.
12.
13.
14.
15.
16.
17.
18.
19.
20.

MONKEY LOVES HIS COOKIES BUT NO WAY IS HE SHARING, SO YOU'LL HAVE TO MAKE SOME OF YOUR OWN!

MONKEY'S MUNCHIES

 ## YOU'LL NEED:

- 125g SOFT BUTTER
- 180g CASTER SUGAR
- 200g SIEVED SELF-RAISING FLOUR
- 1 EGG
- 2-3 DROPS OF VANILLA EXTRACT
- 150g CHOCOLATE CHIPS

 ## ALL YOU NEED TO DO IS:

1. Ask a grown-up to preheat the oven to 180° C or Gas Mark 4.

2. Use a wooden spoon to cream the butter and sugar together in a bowl until the mixture is fluffy.

3. Mix in the egg and vanilla essence.

4. Add the flour and gently mix everything together thoroughly before stirring in the chocolate chips.

5. Place a dessertspoon of the mixture for each cookie onto greased baking trays, giving each one plenty of space to spread out.

6. Ask a grown-up to bake the cookies for 12-14 minutes and take them out to cool.

Remember not to hide your cookies on the top shelf where pandas can reach them!

WASHING BY NUMBERS

WHERE DID PO TRY TO WASH HIS PITS WHILST OUT WITH SHIFU? TO FIND OUT, DO THE SUMS TO SEE WHICH LETTERS GO IN THE SPACES AND THEN FILL THEM IN. THE ANSWER IS AT THE BACK OF YOUR ANNUAL.

14 – 11 = ... H

2 + 7 = ... E

9 + 4 = ... T

15 – 13 = ... P

1 + 6 = ... O

3 + 5 = ... C

12 – 8 = ... F

19 – 14 = ... A

9 + 9 = ... S

13 – 7 = ... D

18 – 17 = ... R

17 – 6 = ... L

13 3 9   2 7 7 11   7 4   18 5 8 1 9 6   13 9 5 1 18

PO'S A-Z OF KUNG FU

NOW PO IS A MASTER, HE KNOWS ALL THERE IS TO KNOW ABOUT THE WORLD OF KUNG FU. READ ON TO SHARE HIS KNOWLEDGE!

 A is for acupuncture, an ancient practice that balances the body's energy flow with fine needles. (It doesn't work that well on pandas, though!)

 B is for Bull, a legendary master whose picture hangs in the Jade Palace's Hall of Warriors.

 C is for China, the birthplace of kung fu.

 D is for dumplings. Shifu had never used them in training before... until he met Po!

 E is for endurance (of which Po has little!)

F is for Furious Five, the greatest kung fu masters in China.

G is for Gauntlet of Wooden Warriors, the series of studded dummies that is Mantis's favourite piece of training equipment.

H is for Hall of Warriors, the sacred room that honours the memories of fallen heroes who used kung fu as a force for good.

I is for incense, burned during meditation to fill the room with a relaxing fragrance.

J is for Jade Palace, where the best kung fu masters live and train.

K is for kung fu, which means 'skill achieved by hard work'.

L is for learning from and listening to… one's master.

M is for Moon Pool, the mystical pool in the Jade Palace that is said to provide answers to the most difficult of questions.

N is for noodles – Po loves them, but not so much that he wants to spend the rest of his life making them!

O is for Oogway, who created kung fu as a defence for the defenceless and who will never be forgotten.

P is for patience, which all masters must have – especially the one who has to train Po!

Q is for Qi, the 'breath' or 'life force' that is the basis of the universe and everything in it.

R is for ring blades, the weapons used by the legendary Grand Masters Twin Weasels. They were sharp enough to cut through any armour and now sit in the Hall of Warriors.

S is for the Scroll that contains the ultimate kung fu secret: the key to limitless power.

T is for the training hall (or kwoon) at the palace, which was built nine hundred years ago for the first instructor appointed by Oogway to train students in kung fu.

U is for universe – every true master should be at one with it during meditation.

V is for venerable masters: those who command great respect, such as Master Oogway and Master Shifu.

W is for Wuxi Finger Hold. Any warrior who can master this move fights to win!

X is for the Xing Yun Jin Cave of kung fu legend, said to be lined with gold and guarded by a seven-toed demon serpent that inspired the training hall's seven-talon rings.

Y is for yellow, associated with royalty in ancient China.

Z is for Zeng, whose loose feather allowed Tai Lung to escape from Chorh-Gom.

WORDS OF WISDOM

OOGWAY MAY BE GONE, BUT HIS SAYINGS WILL BE REMEMBERED FOR YEARS TO COME. SEE IF YOU CAN COMPLETE THESE PHRASES OF HIS BY CHOOSING THE MISSING WORDS FROM THOSE AT THE BOTTOM OF THE PAGE. YOU CAN FIND THE COMPLETED PHRASES AT THE BACK OF YOUR ANNUAL.

1) Nothing is _____

2) Yesterday is _____ tomorrow is a mystery, but today is a gift. That is why it is called the _____

3) You must _____

4) The _____ has brought us the Dragon Warrior!

5) There are no _____

6) One often meets his _____ on the road he takes to avoid it.

7) There is just _____ There is no good or bad.

8) Quit, don't quit. Noodles, don't _____

BELIEVE   UNIVERSE   PRESENT   IMPOSSIBLE

NOODLES   ACCIDENTS   NEWS   DESTINY   HISTORY

92

KUNG FU MASTER

AFTER ALL THAT ONE-TO-ONE TRAINING WITH SHIFU, PO IS AT LAST A KUNG FU MASTER. USE A PENCIL TO COPY THE PICTURE SQUARE BY SQUARE AND DRAW PO.

BEHOLD
THE DRAGON SCROLL

Tigress and Tai Lung faced each other on the bridge. She pounced first and battle commenced, the two exchanging blows even as they hung precariously over the valley. Monkey told Crane and Viper to help her while he and Mantis took care of the ropes. Viper sprang around Tai Lung's neck, but he quickly grabbed her by the throat and Crane had to kick him away.

"Go!" Mantis shouted to Monkey, immediately regretting it as he struggled alone with the ropes. Monkey knew there was no time to waste and executed a powerful kick to Tai Lung's chest, sending him crashing through the bridge's slats. He rushed back to join the others as Mantis jerked the rope so that it whipped their enemy in the face.

Seeing their chance, the Five attacked Tai Lung in a final flurry just before Tigress let the rope bridge drop, sending him plummeting into the misty depths. Their relief was short-lived as, seconds later, Tai Lung appeared behind them. "Shifu taught you well," he growled, "but he didn't teach you everything."

It was late afternoon when Shifu and Po returned to the Jade Palace from their training session. "You have done well, panda," Shifu told his pupil. "Done well? I've done awesome!" Po exclaimed, knocking Shifu off balance with a belly bounce. "The mark of a true hero is humility," said the master, "but yes, you have done awesome." They both laughed as he did a playful punch back, but were shocked into silence when Crane flew in carrying the others and dropped them in an exhausted heap. "Guys!" cried Po, dropping his rucksack and running over.

"We were no match for Tai Lung's nerve attack," Crane gasped. Shifu saw the others were paralysed and, one by one, he released them.
"I thought we could stop him," groaned Tigress.
"He could've killed you," scolded her master.
"Why didn't he?" asked Mantis.
"So you could come back here and strike fear into our hearts. But it won't work!" Shifu declared.
Po wasn't so sure; he was pretty scared.
"You can defeat him, panda," Shifu insisted. "You will have the one thing that no one else has..."

Moments later they were all looking up at it: the Dragon Scroll.
"You really believe I'm ready?" asked Po uncertainly.
"You are, Po," Shifu nodded. He took Oogway's staff from its candlelit rack and held it above his head by the Moon Pool.

Po and the others watched in astonishment as a cloud of peach blossom petals rose up from the surface and whirled up around the carved dragon, loosening the scroll from its mouth. Shifu caught it on the end of the staff and held it out to Po.
"Behold, the Dragon Scroll," he said. "It is yours."
"Wait," Po smiled nervously. "What happens when I read it?"

"No one knows," Shifu replied, "But legend says you will be able to hear a butterfly's wing beat and see light in the deepest cave. You will feel the universe in motion around you." "Whoa! That's cool!" exclaimed Po. "Can I punch through walls? Will I have invisibility?" "Focus. Focus," Shifu said calmly. "Read it, Po, and fulfil your destiny. Read it and become the Dragon Warrior!"

Po took a deep breath and tried to pull the top off the scroll's holder.

"It's impossible to open," he grunted, trying to bite it off. Shifu effortlessly opened it and handed it back.

"Thank you," said Po. "I probably loosened it for you, though."

Po took out the legendary scroll and its golden light bathed his face as he opened it.

"AAAAAAAARGH!" he yelled. The others were almost as terrified as he was.

"It's blank!" Po exclaimed. "Look!" He tried to show Shifu, but the master covered his eyes.

"No! I am forbidden to look upon..." he began. Curiosity quickly got the better of him and he grabbed the scroll.

"Blank?" he gasped. "I... I don't understand."

"Okay, so Oogway was just a crazy old tortoise after all?" asked Po.

"No," Shifu shook his head thoughtfully. "Oogway was wiser than us all."

"Of course I'm not the Dragon Warrior!" scoffed Po. "Who am I kidding?"

"But who will stop Tai Lung?" asked Tigress.

"He'll destroy everything... and everyone," added Crane.

Shifu calmly ordered the Five to evacuate the valley to protect the villagers from Tai Lung's rage.

"What about you, master?" Tigress asked.

"I will fight him," Shifu
replied. "I can hold him
off long enough for
everyone to escape."
"But he'll kill you,"
said Po, alarmed.
"Then I will finally have paid
for my mistake. It is time for
you to continue your journey
without me. I am very proud
to have been your master."
Shifu and his students bowed
to each other solemnly
before Po and the Five left
for the village. Po looked so
heartbroken that Crane kindly
put his wing around him.

Outside the palace, the Five and Po went in different directions to evacuate the villagers. "Look, it's the Dragon Warrior," someone joked, as Po glumly approached his dad's shop. "Hey, Dad," he said.

"Po!" Mr Ping hurried over to hug his son and managed to pull the apron trick again. "Good to have you back, son! I'm sorry things didn't work out. It just... wasn't meant to be. We are noodle folk, broth runs deep through our veins."

Po didn't think so. Sometimes he couldn't believe he was actually Mr Ping's son.

"Po, I think it's time I told you something I should have told you a long time ago," added Mr Ping. Po wondered what on earth he was going to say. "The secret ingredient of my Secret Ingredient Soup!"

"Oh," Po feigned excitement. "The secret ingredient is..." his father whispered, "...nothing!"

"Huh?" gasped Po. "It's just plain old noodle soup?"

"To make something special, you just have to believe it's special," Mr Ping explained. Po gawped at him as everything began to make sense. "There is no secret ingredient..."

As dawn broke the next morning, Tai Lung appeared before Master Shifu outside the palace.

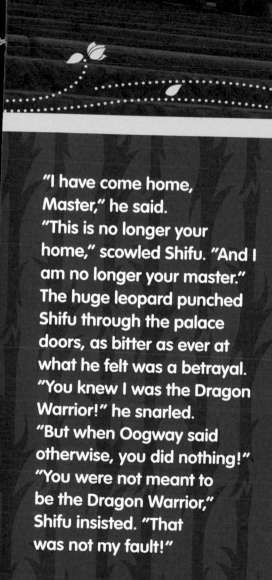

"I have come home, Master," he said.
"This is no longer your home," scowled Shifu. "And I am no longer your master." The huge leopard punched Shifu through the palace doors, as bitter as ever at what he felt was a betrayal. "You knew I was the Dragon Warrior!" he snarled. "But when Oogway said otherwise, you did nothing!" "You were not meant to be the Dragon Warrior," Shifu insisted. "That was not my fault!"

"Who filled my head with dreams?" raged Tai Lung. "Who drove me to train until my bones cracked?" He pulled Oogway's staff from its shrine and used it to pin down Shifu. "Give me the scroll," he demanded.
"I would rather die," said Shifu defiantly. The pair viciously battled each other around the hall, knocking a lantern to the floor and starting a fire.
"All I ever did, I did to make you proud!" cried Tai Lung, charging with his arms aflame. "Tell me how proud you are, Shifu! Tell me!" He punched the master across the floor, sending him crashing into the Moon Pool.
"I have always been proud of you," Shifu said weakly. "It was my pride that blinded me. I loved you too much to see what you were becoming. I'm... sorry."

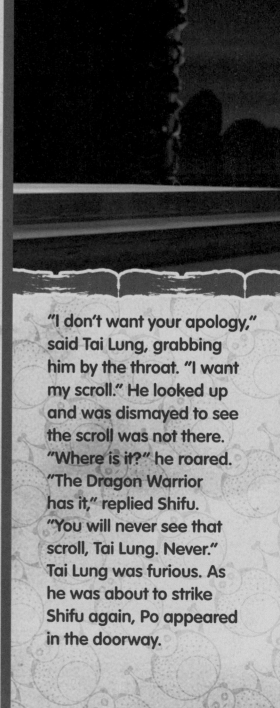

"I don't want your apology," said Tai Lung, grabbing him by the throat. "I want my scroll." He looked up and was dismayed to see the scroll was not there.
"Where is it?" he roared.
"The Dragon Warrior has it," replied Shifu.
"You will never see that scroll, Tai Lung. Never."
Tai Lung was furious. As he was about to strike Shifu again, Po appeared in the doorway.

"Hey!" he called.

"Who are you?" asked Tai Lung.

"Buddy, I am the Dragon Warrior," Po replied, out of breath from climbing the stairs.

"What are you gonna do, big guy?" snorted the leopard. "Sit on me?"

"Don't tempt me," chuckled Po, as he held up the scroll. "No, I'm gonna use this. You want it? Come and get it."

Poor Po didn't even see the punch coming that allowed Tai Lung to snatch the scroll.

Po bounced off a pillar, starting a furious fight that took them rolling down the steps, the scroll passing to and fro between them. "That scroll is mine!" snarled Tai Lung, as the two careered towards the village rooftops whilst still grappling for the scroll. Finally, Po landed in a wok shop and the scroll rolled to a stop in the street. Before Tai Lung could reach it, Po

Tai Lung hurled Po into a fireworks stall. As he turned back, he was astonished to see the panda flying through a firework-filled sky. Po slammed into the leopard, knocking the scroll way up into the mouth of a rooftop dragon, and then he effortlessly scaled the building, just as if he were scrambling up cupboards for cookies.

"The scroll has given him power," gasped Tai Lung. In desperation, he kicked the building so hard that it collapsed.

"Finally," he purred, looming over Po, "the power of the Dragon Scroll is mine!" He snatched the scroll and opened it.

"It's nothing!" he exclaimed in astonishment.

"It's okay. I didn't get it the first time either," said Po. "There is no secret ingredient. Ultimate power isn't gonna be found on a piece of paper. It comes from within."

hid it under an upturned wok amongst some others. The leopard was soon upon him, glaring as he played a shell game with the woks, sliding them around to see if Tai Lung could guess the right one. "Lightning!" he grinned. Tai Lung angrily swiped the woks away and the two continued their fight as the scroll rolled towards the river.

In a fury, Tai Lung went for Po's nerve points.
"Stop it!" Po giggled. "I'm gonna pee!" Tai
Lung tried a double-fisted punch to Po's
belly, but the shockwave made the panda's
arms deliver a powerful strike in return.
"You can't defeat me," panted Tai Lung.
"You're just a big, fat panda!"
In reply, Po grabbed the leopard's finger.
"The Wuxi Finger Hold!" yelped Tai Lung.
"You're bluffing! Shifu didn't teach you that!"
Po flexed his pinky and KA-THOOM! A
mushroom cloud appeared over the
valley as Tai Lung was defeated.

Po received a hero's welcome at last. Villagers
cheered as the Dragon Warrior was reunited with
his father. The Five were there to greet him too.
"Master," said Tigress, bowing
deeply. The others followed.
"Master?" echoed Po in astonishment.

Remembering his own
master, Po hurried to the
palace. He found Shifu lying
lifeless by the Moon Pool.
"Master!" he gasped.
"Po," whispered Shifu, his
eyes fluttering open. "You're
alive! Or we're both dead."
"I didn't die," Po said proudly.
"I defeated Tai Lung!"
"It is as Oogway foretold,"
Shifu smiled in disbelief. "You
are the Dragon Warrior. You
have brought peace to this
valley, and to me. Thank you..."

Shifu's eyes closed again
and he was still.
"No! Master!" cried Po.
"Don't die, Shifu!"
"I'm not dying, you idiot,
ah, Dragon Warrior," said
the master. "I'm simply
at peace. Finally."
Po tried to stop talking, but his
mind soon turned to other things.
"Want to get something
to eat?" he asked.
"Yeah," Shifu sighed. Maybe
he hadn't changed this
big, fat panda after all!

THE END

ANSWERS

PAGE 25

PAGE 26
Master Oogway

PAGE 44

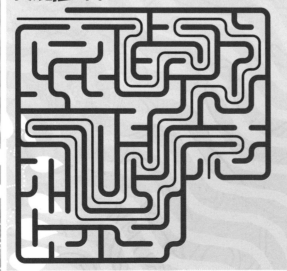

PAGE 47

```
M O N K E Y
    T A I L U N G
D U M P L I N G S
    D R A G O N S C R O L L
    S H I F U
        U R N
```

PAGE 48

PAGE 50
Master Shifu

PAGE 51

OOGWAY

PAGE 66

D	R	A	G	O	N	W	A	R	R	I	O	R	E
R	B	G	Q	M	A	N	T	I	S	Z	E	G	C
A	E	N	O	O	D	L	E	S	R	P	J	N	A
G	N	I	P	R	M	W	R	E	I	R	A	V	E
O	A	L	Y	C	H	A	Z	V	S	E	D	T	P
N	R	P	E	G	N	U	L	I	A	T	E	I	F
S	C	M	K	K	U	N	G	F	U	S	P	G	O
C	B	U	N	K	H	O	U	S	E	A	A	R	Y
R	Z	D	O	Q	T	N	Y	U	Z	M	L	E	E
O	K	E	M	G	Y	A	P	O	W	Z	A	S	L
L	C	I	N	E	W	S	H	I	F	U	C	S	L
L	A	Z	J	G	N	B	P	R	Y	H	E	T	A
B	J	M	O	L	L	Y	O	U	W	U	X	I	V
S	R	O	I	R	R	A	W	F	O	L	L	A	H

PAGE 87

15 chopsticks

PAGE 89
THE POOL OF SACRED TEARS

PAGE 92

1) Nothing is IMPOSSIBLE

2) Yesterday is HISTORY, tomorrow is a mystery, but today is a gift. That is why it is called the PRESENT.

3) You must BELIEVE.

4) The UNIVERSE has brought us the Dragon Warrior!

5) There are no ACCIDENTS.

6) One often meets his DESTINY on the road he takes to avoid it.

7) There is just NEWS. There is no good or bad.

8) Quit, don't quit. Noodles, don't NOODLES.